KINDNESS OF HEARTS

BONNIE KRUM

PAGE PUBLISHING
Conneaut Lake, PA

First originally published by Page Publishing 2022

ISBN 978-1-6624-6363-1 (pbk)
ISBN 978-1-6624-8277-9 (hc)
ISBN 978-1-6624-8276-2 (digital)

Printed in the United States of America

For Angie and Jeremy

Ava woke up excited about her day. She was in kindergarten, and her teacher, Mrs. Applegate, promised a surprise for all the students on Friday if everyone accomplished their weekly assignment on time. Mrs. Applegate was a fun teacher. She always came up with games to help her students learn. Ava liked that she could play and learn at the same time.

Ava waved goodbye to her mom, climbed the three steps up to the school bus, and took a seat next to her sister, Alexa. Alexa was in third grade. Alexa had Mr. Johnson as her teacher this year, but she remembered Mrs. Applegate from when she was in kindergarten. While Ava looked out the window as the bus pulled away and headed for the school, Alexa was busy doing math problems in her head. She wanted to ace the test Mr. Johnson was giving first thing this morning.

Mrs. Applegate was busy organizing things on her desk when the children arrived at her door. She quickly went over to greet them, giving each student a hug and welcoming them to class. She did not hurry but took her time to talk to each student. Everyone waited patiently in line for their turn. Everyone loved Mrs. Applegate's hugs, especially Ava.

Monday morning always started the same. Mrs. Applegate had her students sit in a circle on the rug to sing their "Good Morning" song. Then she picked names from a hat to assign duties for the day. Ava hoped she would get to be the snack helper. She had been waiting for two weeks now to get chosen.

She was the bell ringer once, and the line leader once, but she really, really wanted to be the snack helper. Her friend Laney had been the snack helper two times already! But Mrs. Applegate picked Danny's name from the hat, and now Ava would have to wait again. Ava was learning that being patient was not easy.

8

After they found the right day, month, and year on the calendar and recited the Pledge of Allegiance, Mrs. Applegate announced it was time to talk about their new assignment. All the children clapped. Last week, their project was to build something out of toothpicks and marshmallows. Ava ate marshmallows while she built a big bridge. It was a fun assignment!

Mrs. Applegate went to the chalkboard and wrote the word *kindness*. Then, she asked if anyone could tell her what it meant.

Danny raised his hand. "It means kind," he said.

"Well, yes," said Mrs. Applegate, "but what does *kind* mean?"

Sarah raised her hand. "It means not being mean."

Again, Mrs. Applegate agreed. "Does anyone else have an idea on what kindness means?" she asked.

Ava raised her hand. "Maybe to do something nice," she answered.

"Exactly, Ava," said Mrs. Applegate. "To do something nice for someone else. To show compassion, thoughtfulness, and generosity to someone. To make someone else feel good. So the assignment this week is for you each to show kindness to three different people. You can choose family members, friends, neighbors, or anyone you wish. Be creative. Think of ways to be kind to others. At the end of the week, you will have time to draw pictures demonstrating your acts of kindness, and each of you will have the opportunity to share your pictures and talk about them in class on Friday morning."

Mrs. Applegate also encouraged the children to share an act of kindness in school during the week. She put a big heart in the middle of her bulletin board. She asked the children, "Where does kindness come from?"

Sarah raised her hand again. "It comes from something you do."

"Yes," said Mrs. Applegate, "but why do you do what you do? What makes you show kindness to someone?"

The children all looked at one another, and then Laney raised her hand.

Mrs. Applegate smiled and said, "Laney, where do you think kindness comes from?"

Laney stated, "Kindness comes from the heart!"

Mrs. Applegate asked the children if they agreed with Laney. Everyone raised their hand.

"Yes," said Mrs. Applegate, "kindness comes from the heart." Mrs. Applegate explained that she would add a small heart with the child's name to the big heart on the board each time she noticed someone doing a random act of kindness.

Mrs. Applegate then went on with her lessons for the day.

During math, Jennifer noticed that Stephanie couldn't find her pencil. Jennifer leaned over and handed her one of her extra pencils. Mrs. Applegate noticed this act of kindness and put the first small heart with Jennifer's name on the board. Jennifer felt proud of herself for doing an act of kindness, and Stephanie smiled and whispered, "Thank you."

During snack time, the children enjoyed cheese and crackers and apple juice. Caleb was making silly faces, and everyone at his table was laughing. Mary Sue was watching Caleb when she reached for her juice and accidentally knocked the juice over.

She looked upset and scared. Danny jumped up and grabbed a few paper towels and helped Mary Sue clean up the spilled juice. The teacher poured more juice in Mary Sue's cup and then added another small heart to the board.

18

Before the end of the day, there were five more hearts on the board. Mrs. Applegate said she would add hearts all week for acts of kindness. The children all wanted their name on the board, and they tried to think of ways to show kindness.

The school bell rang, and the children gathered up their backpacks, lunchboxes, and coats. Ava went to the line for students who rode the bus to school. She couldn't wait to get home and tell her mom and dad about her new assignment. Ava told Alexa about her assignment on the way home, and Alexa told Ava she aced the math test. Ava gave her sister a big hug.

23

The next day, Ava woke up to snow on the ground. She ran down the stairs, and Mom told her before she even asked that there would be no school today. Ava ran back upstairs to tell Alexa. They both jumped up and down and raced around the room. Mom made pancakes for breakfast, and afterward, Alexa and Ava put on their coats, boots, and mittens. Mom and Ava's older brother, JT, went outside to shovel the driveway while Alexa and Ava rolled snowballs to make a snowman.

Across the street, Mrs. Grady was attempting to let her small dog out, but she was having difficulty walking in the snow. Ava saw her almost slip and fall. Ava had an idea. She talked to Mom first, and then JT went in the garage and got Ava and Alexa their small snow shovels. By this time, Mrs. Grady had gone back inside. She was older and didn't like the snow much.

The snow made her bones ache. Ava, Alexa, and JT worked hard to clear the snow from Mrs. Grady's sidewalk. Mom helped. They cleared all the snow and made a path for Mrs. Grady to walk her dog. It took a while, and Mrs. Grady watched from her front window. When they were almost done, Mrs. Grady poked her head outside and asked if they would like to come in for a cup of hot cocoa. Ava and Alexa looked pleadingly at Mom, who then replied, "Sure, we would love to, Mrs. Grady." Mrs. Grady made steaming-hot chocolate and added marshmallows, thanking them for their act of kindness in clearing her walkway for her.

The next day, Ava was back in school. She only had a few more days to complete her assignment. She was having trouble thinking of another act of kindness. She wanted her acts to be special, not everyday acts of kindness like sharing her toys with Alexa or helping her brother, JT, with his hockey practice. That afternoon, Mom said they were going to visit Nana. Nana was in the hospital for a few days. She hurt her hip, and doctors wanted her to get some rest and run some tests. Ava loved Nana, and she was sorry Nana had to stay at the hospital.

But she was happy to know there were so many doctors and nurses at the hospital helping Nana get better. Ava had an idea. She talked to Mom, and then she, Alexa, and JT set to work. They measured, poured, and mixed until the batter was ready to make chocolate chip cookies. Then they boxed them up in small boxes. Everyone went to visit Nana. While at the hospital, JT, Alexa, and Ava went around the hospital floor and handed out boxes of cookies to any nurse or doctor they came across and thanked them for helping Nana.

In the evening, Ava was reading her sight word book and happened to look up and out the window. She saw a squirrel run across the yard and several birds sitting on the fence. Snow still covered the ground, and the wind had picked up a bit, making the branches on the trees sway back and forth. All of a sudden, Ava had another idea. She talked to her mom. After dinner, Ava collected a few pine cones from Daddy's woodpile. She took them inside. Mom put peanut butter on a paper plate, and Ava rolled the pine cone over the plate. On another plate, Mom had spread out some birdseed. Ava rolled her pine cone over the birdseed. She made two pine cones with birdseed and two pine cones with just peanut butter. Dad helped her tie strings to the pine cones. Then Ava and her dad put on their coats, boots, and mittens and went outside. Ava walked around the yard and chose different trees on which to hang her pine cones. She hoped the birds and the squirrel would find the treats she made for them.

30

Friday morning, Ava was ready. She had completed three acts of kindness, one for Mrs. Grady, one for the nurses and doctors at Nana's hospital, and one for the animals in her yard. She was excited to tell Mrs. Applegate.

When she arrived at school, the morning was spent hearing about everyone's acts of kindness. Mrs. Applegate was impressed with how much thought went into everyone's assignment. She asked how the children felt after doing their assignment. Laney said she felt good doing things for others. Danny said he felt grown-up doing things for others. Ava said she felt happy after doing something for someone else.

Mrs. Applegate was pleased with their answers. She felt the children really learned about kindness this week. She showed them the big heart on the board. Everyone's name was on the heart multiple times.

Ava looked over and smiled at Laney. Laney had been chosen to be the snack helper again on Thursday, and she knew Ava really wanted to be the snack helper. She told Mrs. Applegate that she wanted to let Ava be snack helper instead. Ava was happy she had Laney for a friend, and Mrs. Applegate put a heart on the board for Laney's act of kindness.

Mrs. Applegate called all the children to come sit in a circle, and then she went to her desk to get a big tote bag. Inside were small brown bags with the children's names on them. She handed each child a bag and told them to open it. Inside were candy hearts and a special gold pin in the shape of a heart. Mrs. Applegate said they could wear the pin to always remind them that kindness comes from the heart.

ABOUT THE AUTHOR

Bonnie Krum, a Maryland native, has been an early childhood educator for thirty years. Her works, including poetry and educational stories, have been published in local newspapers and magazines. Inspired by her four grandchildren and young students, her children's books aim to bring to life the lessons that showcase family relationships and peer-to-peer interactions.

9 781662 482779